THE MAD READER!
MAD STRIKES BACK!
INSIDE MAD!

and *now* . . . AT LAST . . .

UTTERLY MAD

Yes, MAD—the magazine that brought you SUPER-DUPERMAN! PRINCE VIOLENT! and MICKEY RODENT! —is back again with this fourth and absolutely final (until next time) collection, UTTERLY MAD!

Filled with radioactive ideas and dangerous as a three-week-old liverwurst sandwich, UTTERLY MAD presents startling new facts about MELVIN OF THE APES! FRANK N. STEIN! LITTLE ORPHAN MELVIN! and other beloved characters.

Need we say more?

Yes, to those making their first contact with MAD we would like to add that UTTERLY MAD—like its distinguished predecessors—is a book that will change your life by giving you a new outlook and bringing you greater confidence but mainly by leaving you just a little soft in the squash.

UTTERLY

MA

William M. Gaines

ibooks
new york
www.ibooks.net

DISTRIBUTED BY SIMON & SCHUSTER, INC

ibooks, inc.
24 West 25th Street
New York, NY 10010

The ibooks World Wide Web Site Address is:
http://www.ibooks.net

Visit www.madmag.com

ISBN 0-7434-4481-7
First ibooks, inc. printing June 2002
10 9 8 7 6 5 4 3 2 1

Printed in the U.S.A.

CONTENTS

INTRODUCTION
by Grant Geissman

Utterly MAD is the fourth in a new series of 50th–anniversary facsimile reprints—published by ibooks—of the early *MAD* paperbacks.

The original version of *Utterly MAD* (published in November 1956 by Ballantine Books) followed *The MAD Reader*, *MAD Strikes Back!*, and *Inside MAD* (also available in facsimile editions from ibooks). Continuing the successful formula of its predecessors, it featured reformatted material that originally appeared in the twenty-three-issue run of the *MAD* comic book. As with the other books in the series, all of the material in this collection was written by *MAD* creator Harvey Kurtzman, and featured the core group of early *MAD* artists, including Wallace Wood, Jack Davis, and Bill Elder. And for the first time in the series, we finally get to see the work of an important early *MAD* artist named John Severin.

For all the similarities between this book and the three that preceded it, however, there are a number of very important differences. Unlike the earlier books, there is no "celebrity" introduction. There are no creator credits (writer or artist) on the title-page spread. And most significantly, the full title of the book reads "William M. Gaines' *Utterly MAD*."

To fully explain these changes, some background information is required. As discussed in the introduction to *The MAD Reader*, *MAD* began as a 10¢ comic book in October 1952, created by Harvey Kurtzman and published by William M. Gaines under the E.C. Comics imprint. Kurtzman had been doing incredible, groundbreaking work in *MAD*, but after three years he had grown restless and was unsatisfied with the limitations of comic books. What he had been longing to do was to get out of the comic book game and work in the world of magazines—or "slicks," as they were known in the trade. Kurtzman had been entertaining an offer from an editor friend of his at *Pageant*, a highly regarded digest-sized slick. He told Gaines that he was seriously considering accepting the offer and moving on. Gaines, who was firmly convinced that without Kurtzman there could be no *MAD*, made Kurtzman an offer that he ultimately could not refuse: stay, and he could turn his *MAD* baby into a 25¢ slick. Oddly enough, the transition from the comic book to the magazine version of *MAD* roughly coincided with the release of the first *MAD* paperback. In fact, *The MAD Reader* was important enough that it merited a full-page ad in *MAD*'s final issue as a comic book (#23, May 1955).

MAD graduated to the magazine format with its 24th issue in July 1955, selling for "25¢—Cheap!" This was a thrilling time for Kurtzman. He told *MAD* writer Frank Jacobs in the book *The MAD World of William M. Gaines* that "the next day was one of the most exciting times in my life. I ran down to the newsstand and bought a bunch of slick magazines to see what other people were doing. I was scared to death when we abandoned the comic format, and I couldn't sleep wondering whether *MAD* would succeed in its new format." About this period, Gaines told comics historian John Benson, "I don't think there was the kind of excitement over the [*MAD*] comic book that there was later on when Harvey put out issue #24, the first 25¢ book. That made such a splash that we actually went back to press. It wasn't a good idea to go back to press [because of the lag time involved], but the very fact we did it indicates how well the book did."

For all the excitement, though, there were problems. *MAD* was officially a bimonthly, but the time between issues began stretching out to be much longer; the perfectionist Kurtzman just could not seem to stay on top of his deadlines, often insisting that artists draw and re-draw otherwise "finished" articles. And he was pressuring Gaines for more money: not for himself, but to spend on the magazine. Unfortunately, it was money that Gaines didn't have, due to the mid-1950s collapse of the comic book market. Kurtzman's demands for money coupled with his deadline problems did not sit well with *MAD*'s publisher, and the formerly very friendly relationship began to develop severe frostbite.

It all came to a head in 1956 on what Gaines would later refer to as the "fateful Friday." Several days prior, Kurtzman had come to Gaines and demanded a stock interest in the company in order for him to remain on as *MAD*'s editor. Gaines wrestled with this, but ultimately decided to offer Kurtzman a 10% stake in what had always been a family-owned business. He relayed this to Kurtzman's right-hand man Harry Chester, and was quickly put on notice that this was not the magic number—Kurtzman wanted control of the magazine. "Fifty-one percent of the stock?" Gaines asked incredulously. "Yes," replied Chester. In a 1962 letter to the satire fanzine *Smudge*, Gaines wrote, "I immediately called Harvey at his home, repeated my conversation with Chester, and asked if this correctly represented his feelings.

"'Yes,' said Harvey.

"'Fifty-one percent of the stock?,' said I.

"'Yes,' said Harvey.

"'Goodbye, Harvey,' said I.

"'You'll be sorry, Bill,' said Harvey.

"'Goodbye, Harvey,' said I.

"'You don't know what you're doing, Bill,' said Harvey.

"'Goodbye, Harvey,' said I for the third time, and hung up. As of Friday evening, *MAD* had a new editor: Al Feldstein."

Gaines was profoundly hurt over Kurtzman's power play, and to add insult to injury Kurtzman ended up taking with him most of *MAD*'s artists (including Bill Elder and Jack Davis) to go start a competing humor magazine for *Playboy* publisher Hugh Hefner. (This project, called *Trump*, proved to be a high-quality but ultimately star-crossed experiment, failing after only two issues.) While Feldstein picked up the pieces at *MAD* and moved to get the next issue out (and the next, and the next...), Gaines still had a contract with Ballantine for more paperback collections. Although as *MAD*'s publisher he already had full ownership of the material, on the advice of his attorney he inserted his name above the titles of the subsequent books. Gaines also removed the names of Kurtzman and the artists from the title pages, an act that annoyed Kurtzman to no end. Moreover, Gaines had been splitting the royalties on the paperbacks with Kurtzman and the artists, but after their departure he cut them out. Kurtzman felt he was owed the royalties and sued, Gaines countersued, and the matter dragged on until many years later, when Gaines finally agreed to settle. He hadn't mellowed; Gaines moved to resolve the dispute only because he had sold ownership of *MAD* several years before (while retaining his position as publisher) and didn't feel it was fair to drag the new owners into a battle that wasn't theirs. Although Gaines did pay Kurtzman royalties on reprints of his E.C. horror and war stories (and on the later sale of his original E.C. artwork), Gaines told Frank Jacobs in 1972 that "I still wouldn't pay him a dime on *MAD* if I could

"Pop Art" version, late 1960s (Art credit unavailable)

help it." While in later years the two men did manage to bury the hatchet (Kurtzman even came back and did some artwork for *MAD* in the mid-1980s), the old wounds never quite healed.

It is not clear at this late date whether Kurtzman had a direct hand in selecting the material used in *Utterly MAD*, but based on the acrimony between Gaines and Kurtzman at the time, one would suspect not. The material, however, is as strong as ever.

Kicking off the book is Kurtzman's twist on Edgar Rice Burroughs's *Tarzan of the Apes,* "Melvin of the Apes!" (*MAD* #6, August-September 1953, illustrated by John Severin—in his first appearance in this series). Of the story, Kurtzman told John Benson, "I really started getting on target with *Tarzan.* To this very day *Tarzan* is a never-ending source of material for satire and parody. There's a strong element of sex. I mean, the whole idea, the young man who inherits the Greystoke fortune and decides to go back and live with the apes rather than live with civilization. Such nonsense!" Severin's work is again represented in a similar genre parody, "Robin Hood!" (*MAD* #4, April-May 1953). Discussing why Severin was a good choice for these kinds of stories,

Art by Robert Grossman (1975)

Kurtzman said "John Severin had 'acting'; his figures were absolutely realistic, the buttons, the knuckles were right, they moved right, the bone structure was right."

"Book! Movie!" (*MAD* #13, July 1954, illustrated by Jack Davis) is yet another of Kurtzman's trademark "side by side" comparisons, this one having to do with how material in novels gets "sanitized" by Hollywood when adapted for the big screen.

"G. I. Shmoe!" (*MAD* #10, April 1954, illustrated by Wallace Wood) finds Kurtzman taking on the glamorization of war as routinely seen in the comic books of the time. Kurtzman knew whereof he spoke, because his own war comics, *Two-Fisted Tales* and *Frontline Combat* (also published by E.C. Comics), were the first to show war as it really was, specifically avoiding such romanticism.

"Frank N. Stein!" (*MAD* #8, December 1953-January

1954, illustrated by Bill Elder) puts a *MAD* spin on Mary Wollstonecroft Shelley's archetypal horror character, the Frankenstein monster. Kurtzman's focus here is more on the good doctor himself than on his creation. Mel Brooks fans will notice that there are several satiric parallels between Kurtzman's story and Brooks's own 1974 *Frankenstein* movie send-up, *Young Frankenstein*, including the bumbling assistant and the insertion of a sub-par brain into the body of the monster.

"Little Orphan Melvin!" (*MAD* #9, February-March 1954, illustrated by Wallace Wood) puts the Kurtzman spin on *Little Orphan Annie*, one of the most successful and longest-running comic strips of all time. Written and illustrated by Harold Gray, the strip made its debut in 1924. The feature focused on the adventures of a blank-eyed, spunky orphan named Annie who gets plucked out of an orphanage and adopt-

Art by Norman Mingo (1976)

ed by millionaire "Daddy" Warbucks, who would become her mentor and protector. Annie was often given to uttering long, philosophical monologues, a fact Kurtzman takes note of in the very first panel. The strip also came to include Warbucks's sidekicks Punjab (seen here as "Punjoke"), a giant mystic from India, and the Asp ("Gasp") who was black-garbed, sinister, and especially good at doing away with evildoers. Kurtzman uses the name "Melvin" for the main character—a technique he used repeatedly, providing a thread that runs through many of his *MAD* parodies. Unlike much of his other *MAD* work, Wallace Wood's art here leans more to a "cartoony" approach rather than a direct aping of Gray's drawing style.

For "The Raven" (*MAD* #9, February-March 1954), *MAD*'s setting of the Edgar Allan Poe classic, Kurtzman simply handed the poem off to Bill Elder and instructed him to have his way with it. Kurtzman often referred to the "mind-rotting" power of *MAD*, and in this case he may have been more right than he knew, for few readers of this version are able to go back and read the original poem without thinking of Elder's treatment.

No doubt because the original version of *Utterly MAD* weighed in a little on the thin side compared with the earlier books in the series, in 1963 a revised edition was issued with some additional material. "Supermarkets!" (*MAD* #19, January 1955, illustrated by Jack Davis) looks at what was then a relatively recent phenomenon, the "supermarket," a behemoth replacing the small, neighborhood grocery store. "Stagecoach!" and "The Race!" are from *MAD* #29 (September 1956), its sixth issue as a 25¢ magazine and the first issue to come out after Kurtzman's abrupt departure. These two features are unusual in that they were not written by Kurtzman, but were both written and illustrated by Phil Interlandi. Interlandi did about nine of these "Scenes We'd Like to See" pages for the early magazine version of *MAD*, and then went on to a long career doing cartoons for *Playboy*.

Join us next time for *The Brothers MAD*, the last—but not the least—book in this series. "Alice in Wonderland!" "Woman Wonder!" "Shermlock Shomes in The Hound of the Basketballs!" "Black and Blue Hawks!" *HOOHAH!*

Grant Geissman *is the author of* Collectibly MAD, *(Kitchen Sink Press, 1995), and co-author with Fred von Bernewitz of* Tales of Terror! The EC Companion *(Gemstone/Fantagraphics, 2000). He compiled and annotated the "best of" volumes* MAD About the Fifties *(Little, Brown, 1997),* MAD About the Sixties *(Little, Brown, 1995),* MAD About the Seventies *(Little, Brown, 1996), and* MAD About the Eighties *(Rutledge Hill Press, 1999). He compiled and wrote liner notes for* MAD Grooves *(Rhino, 1996), and also contributed the introduction to* Spy vs. Spy: The Complete Casebook *(Watson-Guptill, 2001). When not reading* MAD, *Geissman is a busy Hollywood studio guitarist, composer, and "contemporary jazz" recording artist with 11 highly regarded albums released under his own name.*

UTTERLY MAD

Jungle Dept.: Africa! Wild . . . untamed land where time stands tangled in the jungle! Africa! . . . Home of the fierce Gmowgli Pygmies . . . the terrible Ngambwali Cannibals, and the horrible Ookaballakonga Head Hunters! Also home of the Jungle Apeman . . . an apeman named . . .

MELVIN OF THE APES!

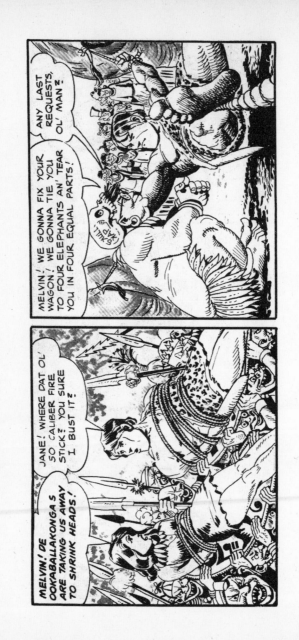

20

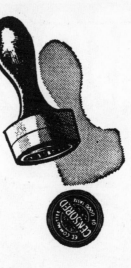

Literature Dept.: Before we launch into our story, we'd like to note that in undertaking this feature, MAD faced the problem that IF we duplicated a typical modern novel in this comic book... we'd be run out of town on a rail! ...So, in the interests of good taste, us Editors have employed the censorship stamp that we picture here!... Wherever you see this stamp, you will know that we of MAD have canceled portions of pictures we have deemed immoral, indecent and mainly bad for business!

—the editors of 'Mad.'

BOOK!

@*☆♏︎Ⓔ!!
EVERY TIME I TRY TO GET A GOOD NIGHT'S SLEEP, MY WIFE PULLS THE COVERS OFFA ME!

LITERATURE DEPT.: WE HAVE ALWAYS WANTED TO COMPARE A BOOK AND THE MOVIE THEY MADE FROM IT! THE FIRST PART OF THIS FEATURE WILL BE A TYPICAL...

Literature Dept.: Before we launch into our story, we'd like to note that in undertaking this feature, MAD faced the problem that IF we duplicated a typical modern novel in this comic book . . . we'd be run out of town on a rail! . . . So, in the interests of good taste, us Editors have employed the censorship stamp that we picture here! . . . Wherever you see this stamp, you will know that we of MAD have canceled portions of pictures we have deemed immoral, indecent and mainly bad for business!

—the editors of 'Mad'

BOOK!
EVERY TIME I TRY TO GET A GOOD NIGHT'S SLEEP, MY WIFE PULLS THE COVERS OFFA ME!
JACK DAVIS
LITERATURE DEPT.: WE HAVE ALWAYS WANTED TO COMPARE A BOOK AND THE MOVIE THEY MADE FROM IT! THE FIRST PART OF THIS FEATURE WILL BE A TYPICAL...

...FIRST, THE BOOK VERSION...

29

ELLEN! YOU'VE GOT THE TABLE SET FOR ME! WHILE I RAN OUT ON YOU... YOU HAVE STAYED FAITHFUL TO ME!... WHILE I WAS READY TO THROW AWAY EVERYTHING FOR A PRETTY FACE... YOU WERE THE TRUE COMPANION AND STAYED FAITHFUL TO ME! GOOD DOG, ELLEN!... GOOD DOG!... CAN YOU FORGIVE ME?
HANDS OFF THAT TABLE! WHEN DID YOU GET BACK? I THOUGHT YOU LEFT FOR GOOD!
THAT TABLE'S SET FOR MY TWIN SISTER HERE WHO'S COMIN' TO LIVE WITH US **FOREVER!**
...AND NOW, THE SITUATION IS IS MORE MISERABLY... HOPELESSLY MISERABLE THAN BEFORE!... WHAT, THEN, IS THE SOLUTION TO THIS MISERABLE STORY? THE SOLUTION IS QUITE SIMPLE!... **END** IT!... THIS MISERABLE HOPELESSLY HOPELESS SITUATION IS JUST PERFECT FOR A **BOOK** ENDING...
EC COMMITTEE CENSORED OF GOOD TASTE
EC COMMITTEE CENSORED OF GOOD TASTE
EC COMMITTEE CENSORED OF GOOD TASTE
END
4

...NOW, THE MOVIE VERSION...

39

42

Hysterical Historical Dept.: Come ye back to ye days of yore! Come ye back to ye merry England! Come ye back to ye days when ye minstrels sang in ye forests of Nottingham! Come ye back to Mandalay where ye flying fishes play! Come ye back to ye days of . . .

ROBIN HOOD!

46

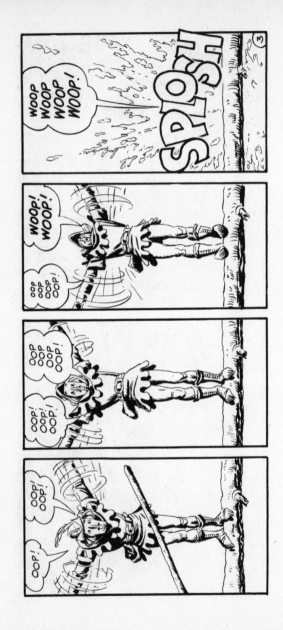

57

59

GO YE AWAY FROM THE DAYS OF YORE! GO YE AWAY FROM MERRY ENGLAND! GO YE AWAY FROM YE DAYS WHEN YE MINSTRELS SANG IN YE FORESTS!

YE MINSTRELS NO LONGER HAVE A SONG...AND YE SKY IS NO LONGER BLUE! AN' YE MORAL TO YE STORY IS...NEVER TRUST A CROOK, EVEN IF IT'S ROBIN HOOD!

War Comics Dept.: For some time, we have been itching to sink our teeth into one type of literature born of the war! . . . We think the time has come! Any similarity between this story and real war is totally accidental! . . . It is with the sincerest respect that we dedicate this lampoon to you real soldiers who have had to put up with the glamorized war comics like . . .

...HEY, JOE! ...YOU GOT CHEWING GUM?

YOU WANT TO SPEAK!...NO DOUBT YOU WANT TO SAY YOU ARE TIRED OF ENEMY WAY OF LIFE...YOU WANT TO WEAR LIP-STICK...YOU WANT TO SHOP IN THE A+P!...YOU WANT TO THROW POP-BOTTLES AT THE UMPIRES!...GO AHEAD, BABY!... WHAT IS IT YOU WISH TO TELL ME?

O.K., BABY! YOU'RE ALL MINE! I GAVE YOU A CHANCE TO HIT ME WITTA GUN-BUTT...BUT NATURALLY, YOU HAVE IMMEDIATELY FALLEN IN LOVE WITH ME SINCE I AM BIG HERO OF THIS STORY!

GOOD WORK, COMRADE! BY CAUSING THEM TO FIGHT EACH OTHER, G.I. SHMOE HAS FIVE BULLETS IN HIS SPINE AND FOUR BULLETS THROUGH HIS HEART! SGT. SQUIRT HAS SEVEN BULLETS IN HIS HEAD AND A BAYONET THROUGH THE GUT! I THINK THEY ARE SUFFICIENTLY WEAKENED FOR CAPTURE!

OH BABY... THE WAY YOU ASK FOR CHEWING GUM... I GET A PRICKLING SENSATION UP AND DOWN MY SPINE!

DON'T TAKE *HIS* GUM, BABY! I'VE GOT INDIAN GUM WITH FREE PICTURE TICKETS IN EACH PACKAGE!

BR... BRUP!

80

Terror Dept.: The scene for this real crazy story is set in the little European town of Veeblefetzer! A figure, bent beneath the weight of a grisly red sack, is seen toiling up the hill towards the castle of Baron Von Stein! . . . Baron Francesco Napoleon Stein . . . known for short as . . .

FRANK N. STEIN!

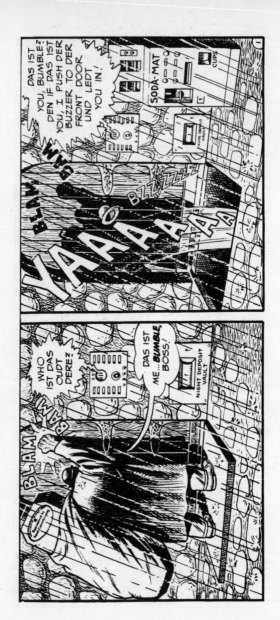

93

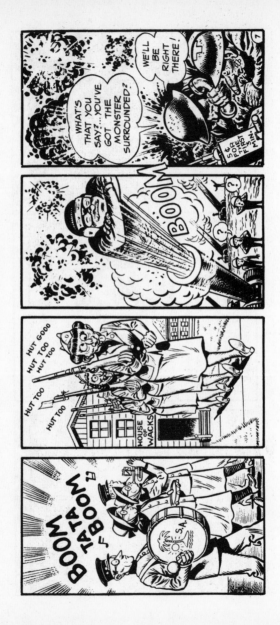

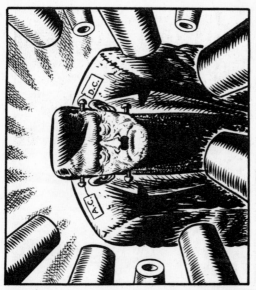

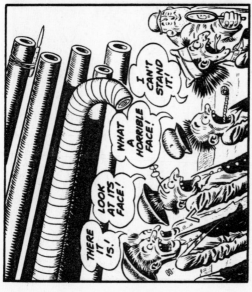

Girl-and-dog-type-story Dept: Take a homeless, lonely orphan-child girl . . . Add a faithful, lovable, highly intelligent mutt-dog . . . and you have a comic strip that'll tug at your heart-strings and loosen your purse-strings! . . . And so we present . . . a girl named Melvin and a dog named Gravel, in . . . .

LITTLE ORPHAN MELVIN!

130

132

Classical Type Comics Dept.: Once upon an evening dreary, while we pondered weak and weary in the Public Libreary, on a comic story plot; while we nodded nearly napping, came an attendant a-tapping, on our head so gently rapping, spoke "That's all the time you've got"!... Ooh were we mad! We howled! We raved! And that's what this story is about...

THE RAVEN

Ah, distinctly I remember it was in the bleak December;
And each separate dying ember wrought its ghost upon the floor.
Eagerly I wished the morrow; vainly I had sought to borrow

From my books surcease of sorrow—sorrow for the lost Lenore—
For the rare and radiant maiden whom the angels name Lenore—

Nameless **here** for evermore.

And the silken, sad, uncertain rustling of each purple curtain
Thrilled me—filled me with fantastic terrors never
felt before;
So that now, to still the beating of my heart, I stood repeating

"'Tis some visiter entreating entrance at my chamber door—
Some late visiter entreating entrance at my chamber door:-

This it is and nothing more."

Presently my soul grew stronger; hesitating then no longer,
"Sir," said I, "or Madam, truly your forgiveness I implore;

But the fact is I was napping and so gently you came rapping,
And so faintly you came tapping, tapping at my chamber door,

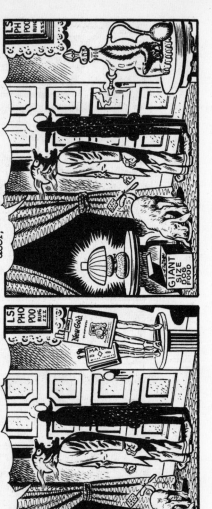

That I scarce was sure I heard you'— here I opened wide the door;—

Darkness there and nothing more.

Deep into that darkness peering, long I stood there wondering, fearing
Doubting, dreaming dreams no mortal ever dared to dream before:
But the silence was unbroken, and the stillness gave no token,

And the only word there spoken was the whispered word, 'Lenore?'
This I whispered, and an echo murmured back the word, 'Lenore!'
Soon again I heard a tapping somewhat louder than before.
"Surely," said I, "surely that is something at my window
lattice;

Merely this and nothing more.

Back into the chamber turning, all my soul within me burning.

Let me see, then, what thereat is, and this mystery explore —
Let my heart be still a moment and this mystery explore; —

"'Tis the wind and nothing more!"

Open here I flung the shutter, when, with many a flirt and flutter,
In there stepped a stately Raven of the saintly days of yore;
Not the least obeisance made he; not a minute stopped or stayed he;

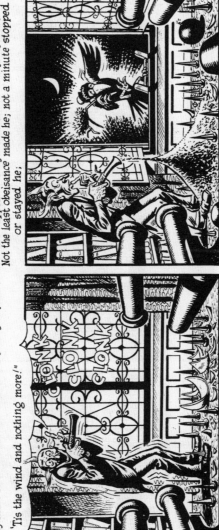

142

But with mien of lord or lady, perched above my chamber door—
Perched upon a bust of Pallas just **above** my chamber door—

Perched, and sat, and nothing more.

Then this ebony bird beguiling my sad fancy into
smiling,
By the grave and stern decorum of the countenance
it wore,

"Though thy crest be shorn and shaven, thou," I said,
"art sure no craven,
Ghastly grim and ancient Raven wandering from
the Nightly shore—

Tell me what thy lordly name is on the Night's
Plutonian shore!"

Quoth the Raven "Nevermore."

Much I marvelled this ungainly fowl to hear
    discourse so plainly,
Though its answer little meaning —little relevancy bore;
For we cannot help agreeing that no living human being

Ever yet was blessed with seeing bird above his chamber door-
Bird or beast upon the sculptured bust above his chamber door,

    With such name as "Nevermore."

But the Raven, sitting lonely on the placid bust, spoke only
That one word, as if his soul in that one word he did outpour.
Nothing farther then he uttered – not a feather then
he fluttered –

Till I scarcely more than muttered "Other friends have flown before -
On the morrow **he** will leave me as my hopes have flown before."

Then the bird said ("Nevermore!")

Startled at the stillness broken by reply so aptly spoken,
"Doubtless," said I, "what it utters is its only stock and store
Caught from some unhappy master whom unmerciful Disaster
Followed fast and followed faster till his songs one burden bore-
Till the dirges of his Hope that melancholy burden bore
Of 'Never—Nevermore.'"

But the Raven still beguiling my sad fancy into smiling,
Straight I wheeled a cushioned seat in front of bird, and bust and door;

Then, upon the velvet sinking, I betook myself to linking
Fancy unto fancy, thinking what this ominous bird of yore —

What this grim, ungainly, ghastly, gaunt, and ominous
bird of yore

Meant in croaking "Nevermore."

This I sat engaged in guessing but no syllable expressing
To the fowl whose fiery eyes now burned into my bosom's
core;

This and more I sat divining, with my head at ease reclining

On the cushion's velvet lining that the lamp-light gloated o'er,
But whose velvet-violet lining with the lamp-light gloating o'er,

She shall press, ah, nevermore!

Then, methought, the air grew denser, perfumed from an unseen censer
Swung by seraphim whose foot-falls tinkled on the **tufted floor.**
"Wretch," I cried, "thy God hath lent thee – by these angels
he hath sent thee

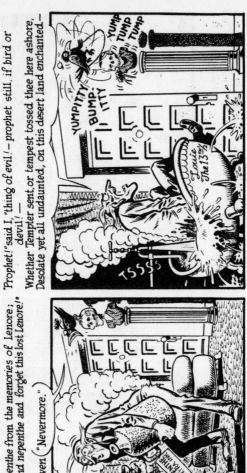

Respite - respite and nepenthe from the memories of Lenore;
Quaff, oh quaff this kind nepenthe and forget this lost Lenore!"

Quoth the Raven ("Nevermore.")

"Prophet!" said I, "thing of evil! - prophet still, if bird or
devil! -

Whether Tempter sent, or tempest tossed thee here ashore,
Desolate yet all undaunted, on this desert land enchanted -

On this home by Horror haunted - tell me truly, I implore —
Is there -**is** there balm in Gilead?- tell me -tell me, I implore!"

"Prophet!"said I", thing of evil! - prophet still. if bird
or devil!
By that heaven that bends above us - by that God we
both adore —

Quoth the Raven ("Nevermore."

151

Tell this soul with sorrow laden if, within the distant Aidenn,
It shall clasp a sainted maiden whom the angels name Lenore —

Clasp a rare and radiant maiden whom the angels name Lenore."

Quoth the Raven ("Nevermore.")

"Be that word our sign of parting, bird or fiend!" I shrieked, upstarting—
"Get thee back into the tempest and the Night's Plutonian shore!
Leave no black plume as a token of that lie thy soul hath spoken!

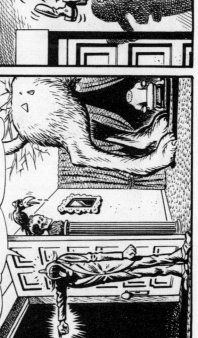

Leave my loneliness unbroken!—Quit the bust above my door!
Take thy beak from out my heart, and take thy form from off my door!"
Quoth the Raven "Nevermore."

And the Raven, Never flitting, **still** is sitting, **still** is sitting
On the pallid bust of Pallas just above my chamber door;
And his eyes have all the seeming of a demon's that is
dreaming,

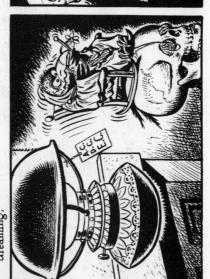

And the lamp-light oer him streaming throws his shadow on the floor;
And my soul from out that shadow that lies floating on the floor

Shall be lifted – nevermore!

The American Scene Dept.: Since we started our "American Scene" series, we have received a virtual flood of letters and telegrams! . . . All kinds of letters and telegrams! By George! . . . We sure wish the finance company'd stop sending us letters and telegrams! . . . Our American Scene for today will be . . .

SUPERMARKETS!

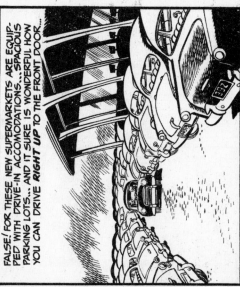

BOY!.. REALLY WONDERFUL! ...GEE!.. SAY!...THERE'S A PARKING SPACE...JUST A LITTLE WAYS AHEAD...

...YES SIR!... WONDERFUL! ...PRACTICALLY RIGHT UP TO THE VERY FRONT DOOR! ...SURE IS CROWDED TODAY!

...YES SIR! IT SURE IS WONDERFUL, THE PARK-ING LOT AND EVERYTHING! ...STILL NO PARKING SPACE!

WELL...PRACTICALLY RIGHT UP TO THE FRONT DOOR! ...OF COURSE YOU HAVE TO FIND A PARKING SPACE...

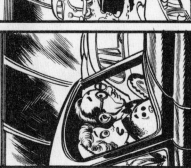

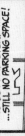
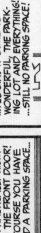
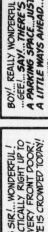

BUT IT ISN'T TOO BAD!... THE HOT ASPHALT OF THE PARKING LOT BRINGS NATURAL FORCES INTO PLAY THAT SOON DEADEN ALL SENSATIONS OF PAIN IN YOUR FEET!... FINALLY... YOU ARRIVE AT THAT OL' FRONT DOOR...

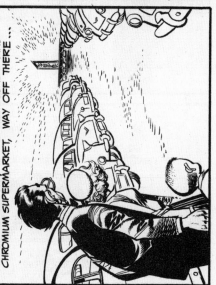

YOU FINALLY PARK THE CAR... GET OUT... STRETCH! ...AND SO, THERE YOU ARE, AND THERE, GLEAMING IN THE FAR DISTANCE, IS THE NEW GLASS AND CHROMIUM SUPERMARKET, WAY OFF THERE...

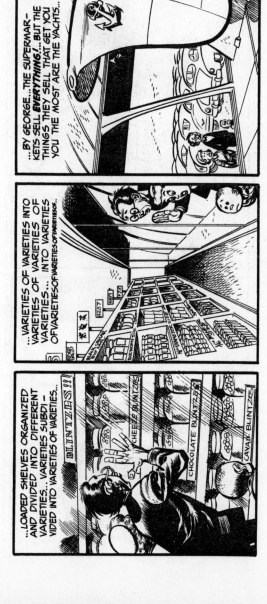

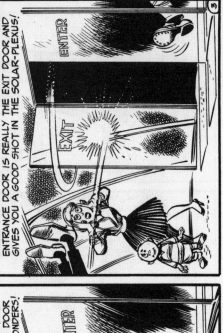

...YES, WONDERS...LIKE THE ENTRANCE DOOR WHICH TAKES YOUR BREATH AWAY...MAINLY SINCE THE ENTRANCE DOOR IS REALLY THE EXIT DOOR AND GIVES YOU A GOOD SHOT IN THE SOLAR-PLEXUS!

AND...LIKE THE INDIAN SPRINGS TO HIS PONY TO DO BATTLE, FIRED BY THE WAR DANCE... SO DO YOU SPRING FOR THE MECHANICAL ENTRANCE DOOR TO DO PURCHASING, FIRED BY THESE WONDERS!

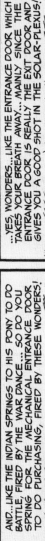

A LUMP IS IN YOUR CHEST AT THE PERFECTION OF IT ALL... HOWEVER, NOTHING IN THIS WORLD IS PER-FECT... AND IF YOU TOOK A SECOND LOOK...YOU'D NOTICE THAT ONE OF THE WAGON'S WHEELS STICKS!

SKWEEE

HOWEVER, POOR FOOLS, YOU DO NOT SEE THE HAND-WRITING ON THE WALL AND YOU MARCH INSIDE WHERE A SHINY CHROME-PLATED SHOP-PING WAGON AWAITS YOU...FREE FOR THE USING!

SEA FOO

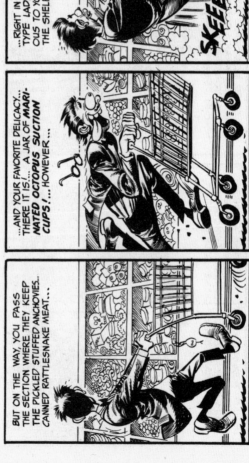

...IT'S *TWO* TYPE LADIES WHO STAND OBLIVIOUS TO YOU...SHOPPING WAGONS BLOCKING THE AISLE! AND NOW WE COME TO THE MOST PERILOUS ASPECT OF SUPERMARKETS... *SHOPPING WAGON JAM.!*

YAIATA YAYTER YAPPA
YATTA YAYTER
YIP YIP YOTTER
YAP YITT!

SUCCESS!... YOU BREAK, RUNNING FREE, LITTLE KNOWING THAT UP AHEAD, THE WORST IS YET TO COME, FOR IF THERE'S ANYTHING WORSE THAN THE TYPE LADY WHO STANDS OBLIVIOUS TO YOU...

172

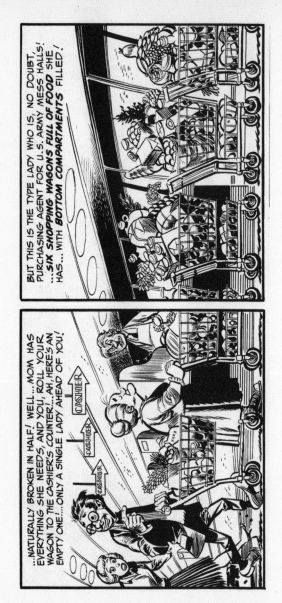

...NATURALLY BROKEN IN HALF! WELL... MOM HAS EVERYTHING SHE NEEDS, AND YOU, ROLL YOUR WAGON TO THE CASHIER'S COUNTER!... AH, HERE'S AN EMPTY ONE!... ONLY A SINGLE LADY AHEAD OF YOU!
CASHIER
CASHIER
CASHIER
BUT THIS IS THE TYPE LADY WHO IS, NO DOUBT, PURCHASING AGENT FOR U.S. ARMY MESS HALLS! ...**SIX SHOPPING WAGONS FULL OF FOOD** SHE HAS... WITH **BOTTOM COMPARTMENTS** FILLED!

THE CASHIER IS REGISTERING THE PACKAGES!...NOTHING CAN GO WRONG NOW...*MAYBE*... BECAUSE AT THE LAST MINUTE, MOM REMEMBERS SHE FORGOT TO PICK UP A BOTTLE OF CHIVES!

OOPS! THE WAGON YOU HAVE SCRUNCHED YOUR WAGON INTO ISN'T EMPTY!...IT STILL HAS A COUPLE PACKAGES AND A LITTLE KID WHO IS FORTUNATELY CUSHIONED BY A MIRANGUE PIE!

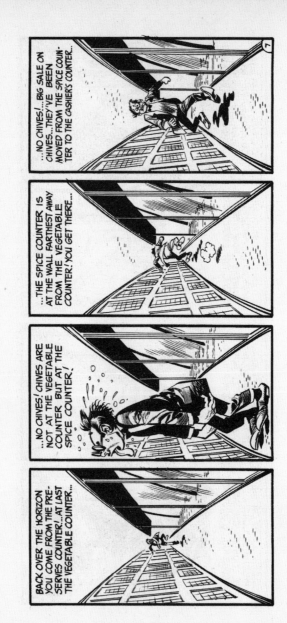

BACK TO THE NEW SUPERMARKET ON THE EDGE OF TOWN, YOU SAY? *OF CUSS NOT!*... BACK TO MR. FURD'S GROCERY STORE...WHERE YOU CAN SQUE-EZE THE BARE ROLLS TO SEE IF THEY'RE FRESH!

AND SO, OFF YOU GO INTO THE SUNSET, MARVELING AT THE ORGANIZATION....THE COMFORT...THE SHEER WONDER OF IT ALL!...AND YOU JUST CAN'T WAIT TO GO BACK THE NEXT DAY!

Scenes We'd Like to See

STAGE COACH

HOLLYWOOD DEPT.

HOLLYWOOD DEPT.

Scenes We'd Like to See

THE RACE

And now, for you MAD readers, an important, astounding, fantastic, dull announcement. We the editors are pleased to announce that a collection of MAD stories have been reprinted in a pocket-book-size edition entitled "The MAD Reader" (after you). For this collection, we have selected the cream of the crop (or the dregs of the earth, whichever the case may be). Yes . . . MAD is marching forward along the victorious path, striding to greater heights, making inroads, as ever, towards destroying minds.

This nauseating little package can be purchased for a trifling 35c. Don't be a cheapskate . . . the object of scorn and ridicule. Scrape up this miserable 35c. We don't question where you get the money . . . whether it's hot or not.

For long hours of enjoyment and happiness, get this book. For the pleasure and entertainment of your friends, get this book. But mainly for the loot we make from the sale of each copy, get this book. Buy The MAD Reader! Buy The MAD Reader! Buy The MAD Reader! Buy The MAD Reader! Buy The MAD Reader! Buy The MAD Reader! Buy The MAD Reader! . . . (We're burning it into your brain, by George!)

Now go out to your drugstore, your newsstand, your candy store, anyplace they sell pocket-books, and buy . . . *buy* . . . BUY . . . the Farmer's Almanac. There's a useful magazine.

The MAD Reader

Original ad for The MAD Reader, *from MAD's final issue as a comic book (#23, May 1955)*

Also available from ibooks:

The MAD Reader

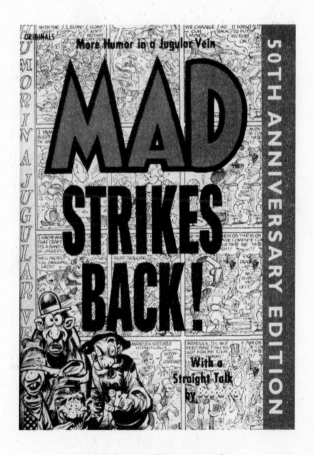

MAD Strikes Back!

From ibooks—

The *MAD* Reader
***MAD* Strikes Back!**
Inside *MAD*
Utterly *MAD*
The Brothers *MAD*